First American Edition 2006
by Kane/Miller Book Publishers, Inc.
La Jolla, California

First published in India in 2000 by Tulika Books
© 2000 Tulika Publishers, Chennai, India.

Library of Congress Control Number: 2006920747
Printed and bound in China
2 3 4 5 6 7 8 9 10

ISBN: 978-1-933605-10-4

KALI
and the Rat Snake

STORY BY
Zai Whitaker

ILLUSTRATIONS BY
Srividya Natarajan

Kane/Miller
BOOK PUBLISHERS

WORDS to DISCOVER

Rupees – The basic unit of currency in India.

Idli – Most often eaten at breakfast or for a snack, idli are small steamed patties made of rice and lentils.

Mixture – A crunchy snack mixture, usually consisting of noodles, mung beans and peanuts.

Irula – Irulas are an indigenous tribal people living throughout Southern India (including Tamilnadu). The Irula have traditionally made their living as snake catchers.

Palmyra – A tall palm tree. Palmyra leaves are used for thatching and weaving.

The rat snake
is called **Sarai Pambu**
in Tamil, the language
of Tamilnadu.

Kali walked along the thorny forest track.
He walked as slowly as he could. He was
on his way to school.

Kali's father was one of the most famous snake catchers among the Irula tribe. He had caught over a hundred cobras just this monsoon and bought many good things for the family. The snake cooperative paid 150 rupees for each poisonous snake. They took out the poison from the snakes to make anti-venom serum. When Kali went snake catching with his father, his legs worked as fast as machines. But now, on the way to school, they slowed down.

"I hate school," he told the bushes as he walked slower and slower, "and school hates me." The bushes did not seem to understand or feel sorry for him. "It's been two months since I started school, and I don't have a single friend. I get the feeling the other kids think Irulas are weird."

On the first day of school, each student had to stand up and tell the whole class three things: his or her name, the name of their village, and what their father did. "My name is Ramu, my village is Meloor, and my father is a bus conductor."

Then came "Selvi, Orathoor, postman."

When it was Kali's turn, he felt very proud. "I am Kali, my village is Kanathoor, and my father is a snake catcher." The children giggled and nudged one another, as if he had said something silly.

For the first time in his life, Kali did not feel proud of being an Irula. He wished he were just like the others, an ordinary boy with a bus conductor father.

That was two months ago. Kali was getting used to things, but it was hard, and his walk to school grew slower and slower.

Kali reached the school gate as the bell was ringing.

As usual, he sat in the back row, alone. He wished
he had friends. He wished he could fail and
be asked to leave school. Failing wasn't easy
though. However badly he tried to do his work,
the teacher was always happy with him.

This morning they had math and writing, and
then it was break time. The children rushed
outside to have their snack. Some had idli,
others had mixture, a slice of bread, or two
or three biscuits. Kali opened his snack box.
Oh no! Fried termites! His favorite, actually, but
what if someone saw?

He'd have to hide. He sat on the wall, far away from all the others,
and finished his snack. Termites didn't taste as good here as they
did at home. Kali worried, "Suppose someone comes near me?
Suppose someone asks what I've brought?"

The bell rang. Break was over. They had the same teacher, but a different subject – English. They had to write the English alphabet on their slates. The teacher walked around the room with a stick, hitting the hands that made mistakes.

"Lucky," thought Kali. Lucky that they could upset the teacher! He, too, would try and make a mess of his slate.

The teacher stood in front of Kali. But instead of a swish of the stick, he got a pat on the back. The teacher held up Kali's slate for the class to see. "Here! This is the kind of work I want to see from everyone," he said.

Now the others would hate him more than ever. Kali could hear the whispering in the classroom. He'd never have friends at school.

Just then, something happened in the room. At first, Kali didn't understand. Arms and legs flew, bodies ran, tumbled over each other, fell, and ran some more. There were shouts from all directions, "Help! Help! Teacher, help!" But the teacher was under his desk. Eyes and hands pointed to the ceiling. Now Kali understood.

There, on the roof, was a large rat snake. It probably wanted the rats on the roof tiles, but it had taken a wrong turn and come into the classroom instead.

Kali's father said that sometimes snakes smelled humans and mistook them for rats. Maybe this one thought, "Wonderful, here's a roomful of rats!"

The rat snake was wrapped around a Palmyra beam on the ceiling. It must have been surprised by all the excitement. Slowly, more and more of its body uncoiled from the beam. Kali, looking up, knew what was going to happen next. And it did.

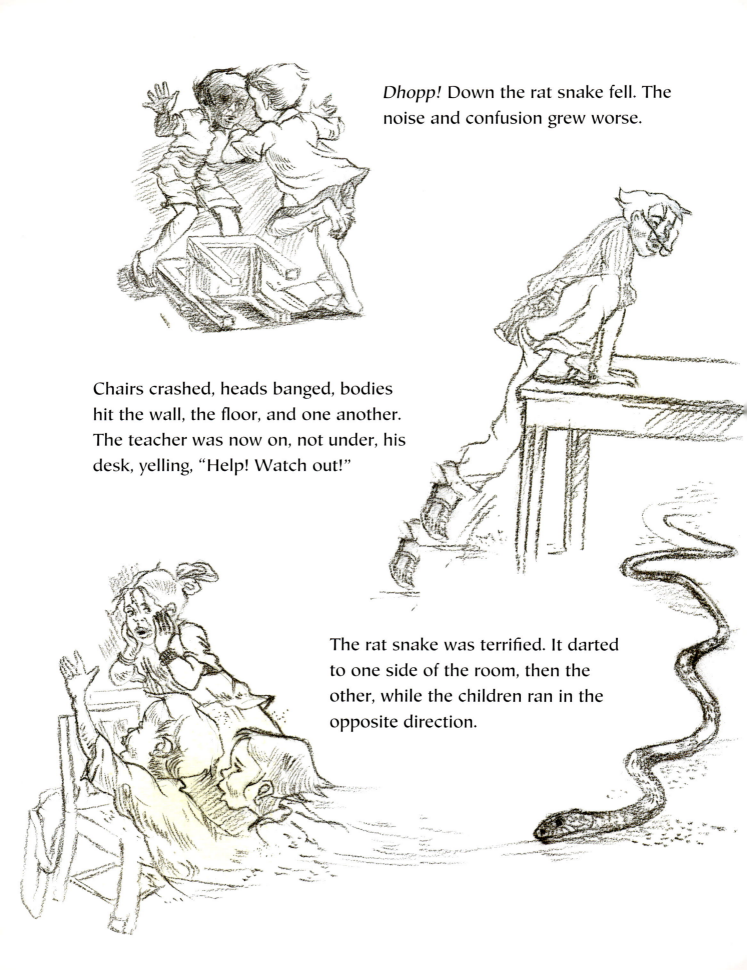

Dhopp! Down the rat snake fell. The noise and confusion grew worse.

Chairs crashed, heads banged, bodies hit the wall, the floor, and one another. The teacher was now on, not under, his desk, yelling, "Help! Watch out!"

The rat snake was terrified. It darted to one side of the room, then the other, while the children ran in the opposite direction.

For a few seconds, Kali was too surprised to do anything. His people, the Irulas, always went towards snakes, not away from them. Had everyone gone crazy? He walked slowly to where the snake was and reached out his hand. Suddenly, the room grew still. There was no sound, no movement. All eyes were on Kali. The six-foot-long snake reared back like a horse, opened its mouth wide, and struck. Luckily, it missed Kali's hand.

"The bite of a big rat snake is very painful," was the thought that went through Kali's mind as he grabbed the snake behind its head. His other hand gripped its long, muscular body. Soon, Kali was all wrapped up in snake.

Kali thought he would find a big bag to put the rat snake in. He'd take it home to his father. The Vandalur Zoo near Chennai paid a good price for rat snakes. He could buy his baby sister a new dress…

But what was that noise? What was happening? Was there another snake in the room? Confused, Kali looked up.

Everyone was clapping and cheering and chanting, "Ka-Li! Ka-Li! Thank-you!" It was wonderful. Kali's eyes filled with tears of joy. He grinned, and the clapping grew louder.

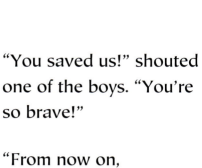

"You saved us!" shouted
one of the boys. "You're
so brave!"

"From now on,
sit next to me!"

"No, me!"

And the children started
quarrelling about who Kali
would sit next to.

"Who taught you to be so brave?" asked Ramesh,
the class bully.

"What do you need? We'll get you whatever you want.
You saved our lives!"

"Well, what I want now," Kali replied, "is a bag – a big bag, to put
him in."

Ten children ran off in ten different directions to find bags. The others looked
at Kali with admiration. Out of the corner of his eye, Kali saw the teacher
climb down off his desk.

He walked up to Kali, but he was careful not to get too close. "Silly children," he scolded. "Why did you get so scared? How ridiculous, running all over the place just because of a non-poisonous snake!"

The teacher walked back to his desk. As soon as his back was turned Kali and the other children grinned at one another…secret grins, the kind that friends use.